The Bully Stop

By

DJ Annie Red

Illustrated by Sylvia Sealy

The Bully Stop

© 2017 by DJ Annie Red

Brown Girls Publishing, LLC www.BrownGirlsBooks.com

ISBN: 978-1-944359-62-1 (ebook)

978-1-944359-63-8 (paperback)

First Brown Girls Publishing LLC trade printing

Manufactured and Printed in the United States of America

The Bully Stop

No, you won't. No, you won't bully me.

I'm working hard to be the best that I can be!

No, you won't. No, you won't bully me.

I know what you're doing comes from your

insecurity.

No me vas intimidr.

Yo estoy trabajando duro y hago

lo mejor que puedo!

Lo que tu haces viene de tu inseguridades.

You bully everyone, make them feel sad.

Being super mean, making everyone mad.

I see you pointing in the cafeteria

All you're trying to do is make me feel inferior.

Tu intimidar a muchas personas y los haga sentir triste.

Te veo en la cafeteria,

tu intentas hacerme sentir inferior.

Sticks and stones do break bones.

But words can hurt, too.

That's why it's important to treat someone

how you want them to treat you.

Palos y piedras rompen huesos, pero palabras

pueden doler tambien.

Por eso importante tartar a alguien

como tu quieres que te tartan a ti.

I am just a kid in this world, trying to find my way.

No need to hurt me, how about we just play?

Soy solo un nino en este mundo,

tratando de econtrar mi camino.

No hay necesidad de lastimarme

Mejor juguemos?

Just because you have disabilities,

doesn't mean you have no abilities.

We're all the same inside, no matter what we do.

So don't bully just because someone is not like you.

Solo porque usted tiene discapacidad

no significa que no tenga ninguna habilidades.

Nosotros todos somos iguales no importa lo que hagamos.

No intimidar solo alguien no es como tu.

You can wear your garb,

you can wear your scarves.

We're all still the same.

You can wear a hat, different clothes,

or have a funny-sounding name.

Tu puedes cubrirte la cabeza,

puedes usar una bufanda.

Nosotros todavia somos iguales.

Puedes usar un sombrero y

ropa diferente or tiener

un nombre con acento diferente.

Cause when you bully,

you're the smaller one, the not-so-funny one,

the one who loses in the end.

When you bully, you hurt others and

no one wants to be your friend.

Cuanda tu molestas a alguien,

tu eres el mas pequeno no eres

muy gracioso y pierdes al final.

Cuando tu molestas y haces dano a

otros nadie quiere ser tu amigo.

No, you should not be a bully,

not on any day.

Always remember,

we are all unique in our own way.

Tu no debes de nunca intimidar.

Recuerde todos somos unicos en nuestra manera.

No, you won't.

No, you won't bully me.

I'm working hard to be the best that I can be.

No me vas a intimidar.

Yo estoy trabajando duro y hago

lo mejor que peudo!

Are you being bullied?

Tell an adult!

Visit www.Safekids.com

Or

www.StopBullying.gov

DJ Annie Red

DJ Annie Red is an eight-year-old Award-winning DJ from Brooklyn, NY. She is a recipient of the 2017 Danny Glover Power of Dreams Music Star Award.

She is also a songwriter and rapper. Her music is available on SoundCloud and Youtube. Her songs include "No, You Won't Bully Me," "DaBoss," and "Give Me a Clean Heart." She is an anti- bullying ambassador, spreading her message throughout the world. You can find her work on www.DJAnnieRed.com.

She has performed with UniverSoul Circus, International Arts Festival and has been featured on various cable TV shows.

Made in United States
Orlando, FL
01 August 2022

20452281R00015